Daddy and ME

A Grosset & Dunlap **ALL ABOARD BOOK**®

With love to George—C.D.
To Chris Green, for being such a wonderful daddy—E.H.

Library of Congress Cataloging-in-Publication Data
Daly-Weir, Catherine.
  Daddy and me / by Catherine Daly-Weir ; photographs by Elizabeth Hathon.
     p. cm. — (All aboard books)
    Summary: Pictures and text relate some of the many things that fathers do with their children, from teaching them to cook to taking them fishing.
    [1. Father and child—Fiction.] I. Hathon, Elizabeth, ill. II. Title. III. Series: Grosset & Dunlap all aboard book.
PZ7.D175Dad 1999
[E]—dc21

99-10942
CIP

ISBN 0-448-41964-5   A B C D E F G H I J

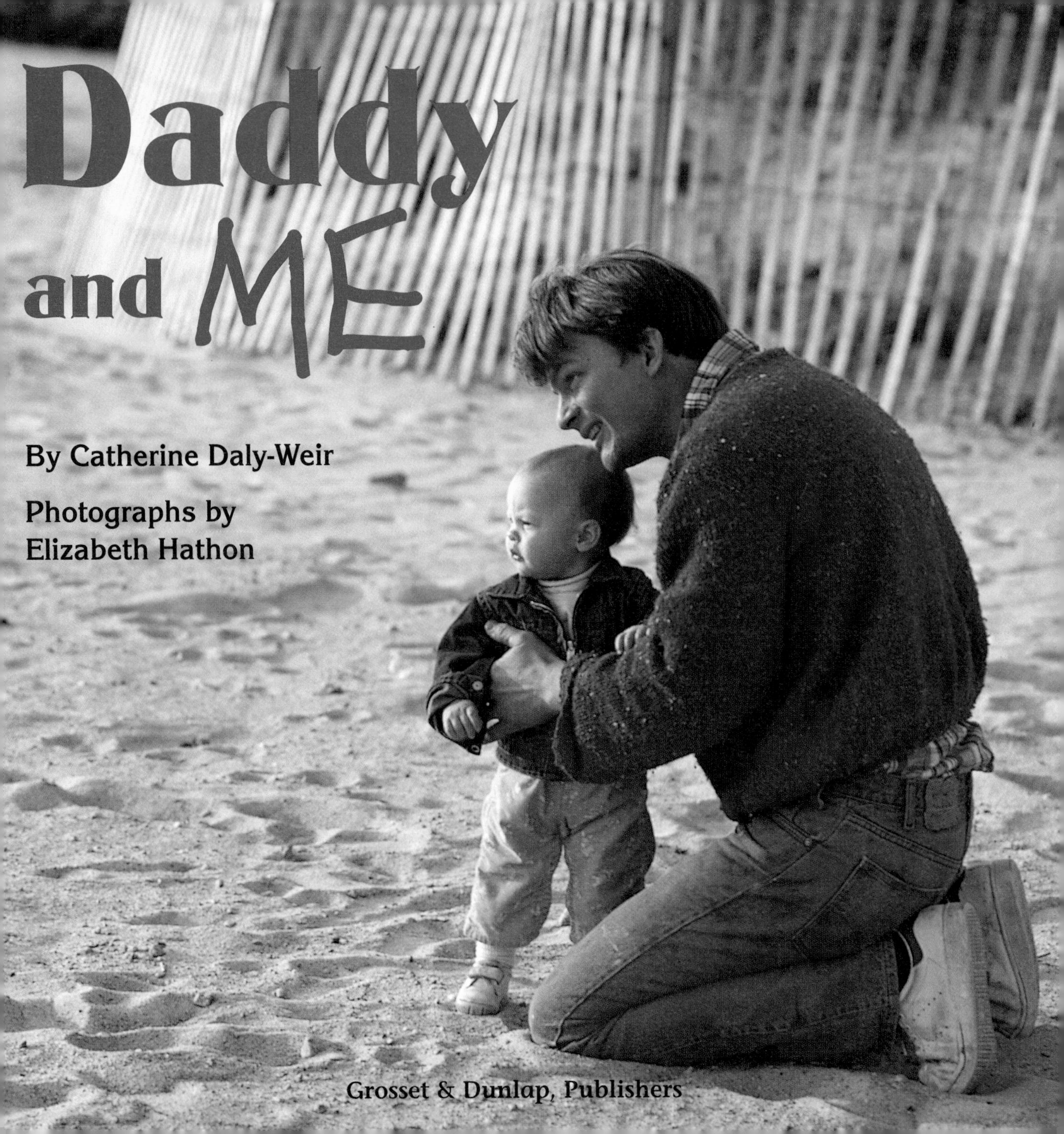

Daddy and ME

By Catherine Daly-Weir

Photographs by
Elizabeth Hathon

Grosset & Dunlap, Publishers

Daddies are very important people. They are loving and gentle. Way back when I was a baby, my daddy took care of me. He would give me baths, feed me, and play with me.

Daddies are good at thinking up fun things to do.

Our daddy takes us fishing. We're the crew and daddy is the captain.

And my daddy and I love to go to baseball games. I bring my glove just in case a foul ball comes our way.

My daddy lifts
me up high so I
can pretend to
be a monkey.

I ride bikes with my daddy. We never forget to wear our helmets.

Our daddy chases us...

then we chase our daddy!

We paint pretty pictures together. And daddy never gets mad if I get paint on his shirt!

Sometimes we pick flowers together.

Daddies like to play pretend.
Today we are world-famous ballerinas.

Daddies are good teachers.
My daddy is teaching me how to cook.
We're making a yummy pizza for Mommy.

I'm learning how to play baseball. My daddy says I'm going to be the next Mark McGwire!

Daddies are big and strong.

But sometimes they need a little help taking home the Christmas tree...

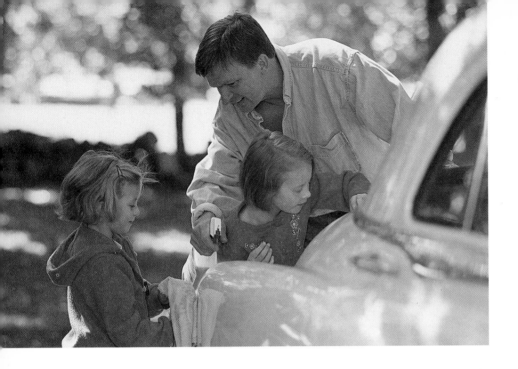

washing the car...

digging in
the garden...

painting
the fence...

mowing the lawn.

Daddies do so many important things.

My daddy cuts my hair. Just a trim please, Daddy.

My daddy makes sure I get on the school bus safely every day.

And mine picks me up from school and asks me how my day was.

My daddy loves
to read to me...

...so does ours, but
sometimes he gets
a little sleepy.
Wake up, Daddy!

My daddy tells me funny jokes to make me laugh.

And my daddy is always there to kiss my boo-boos and make them better.

My daddy takes me shopping. We go to the fruit market. Oranges are my favorite.

Then he helps me pick out my new sneakers.

And when I'm tired after a long day, he puts me on his shoulders...

...and carries me home.

I love my daddy!